Hand in Hand

Rosemary Wells

HENRY HOLT AND COMPANY

NEW YORK

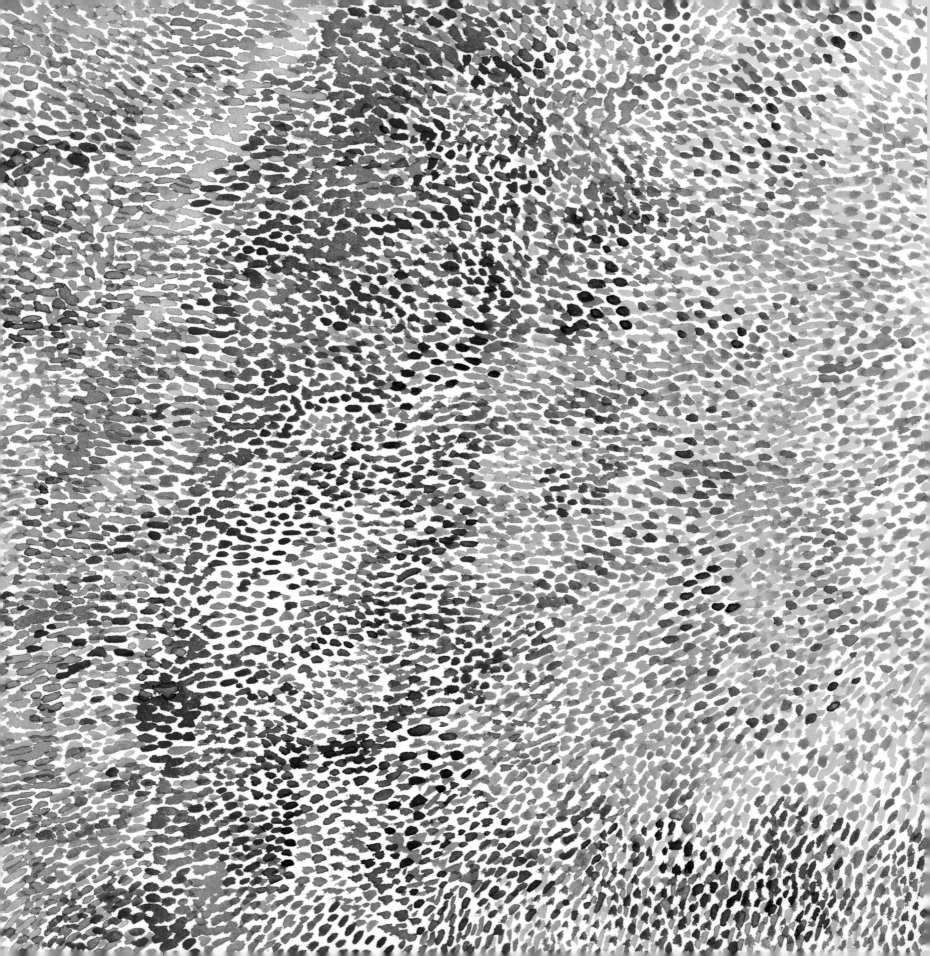

 Be my teacher
from day one.

Be my sky, my moon,

my sun.

My first talker.

My first walker.

My first feeder.

My first reader.

My best playmate.

Midnight staymate.

Make me steady.

Make me strong.

Let me know
my right
from wrong.

Forgiving

Please and Thank You

Praising

Sharing

Helping

Truth Telling

Giving

Kindness is our daily bread;

gentle words, our feather bed.

Lionhearted, we two are.

Be my lighthouse,

my north star.

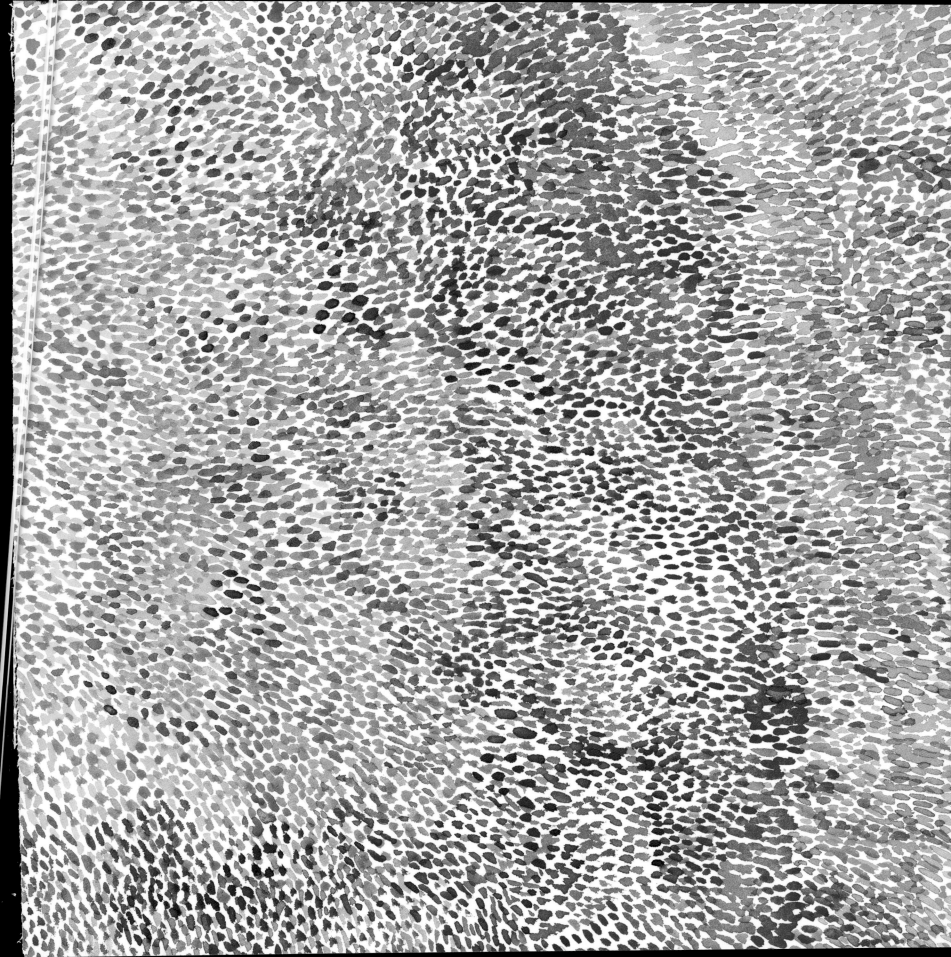

For Merritt Stites
—R. W.

Henry Holt and Company, LLC
Publishers since 1866
175 Fifth Avenue, New York, New York 10010
mackids.com

Henry Holt® is a registered trademark of Henry Holt and Company, LLC.
Copyright © 2016 by Rosemary Wells
All rights reserved.

Library of Congress Cataloging-in-Publication Data is available.
ISBN 978-1-62779-434-3

Our books may be purchased in bulk for promotional, educational, or business use.
Please contact your local bookseller or the Macmillan Corporate and Premium Sales Department
at (800) 221-7945 ext. 5442 or by e-mail at MacmillanSpecialMarkets@macmillan.com.

First Edition—2016 / Designed by April Ward

Printed in China by RR Donnelley Asia Printing Solutions Ltd., Dongguan City, Guangdong Province

1 3 5 7 9 10 8 6 4 2

FROM DAY ONE,

you are your child's first teacher.

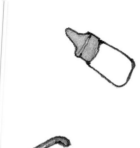

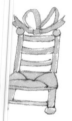

Talk! Play! Read!

Give praise and encouragement.

Share quiet moments every day of the year.

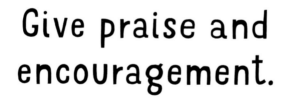